THE LANTERN'S SHADOW

ALENA JAMES

Copyright © 2025 by Alena James

Published in Australia by Crimson Dove Press

Cover design by MiblArt

All rights reserved. No part of this publication can be reproduced, stored in a retrieval system or transmitted, in any form or by any means without the prior written permission of the publisher, nor be otherwise circulated in any form of binding or cover other than that in which it is published and without a similar condition being imposed on the subsequent publisher.

This book is a work of fiction. Any similarities to that of people living or deceased are purely coincidental.

Alena James

The Lantern's Shadow

ISBN: 978-0-6457158-5-9

A catalogue record for this book is available from the National Library of Australia

Dear Reader,

Some stories burn quietly, waiting for their moment.

The Lantern's Shadow is one of those tales. It's a story about warmth found in unexpected places, about courage that flickers even when the world grows cold. Saree and Levi have lingered in the corners of the Mistwalker world, and this Solstice, they stepped forward to tell their part.

This novella lives between *The Mage's Destiny* and *The Mistwalker's Curse*, books 2 and 3 in the Mistwalker Series, when the world is holding its breath and the snow has not yet melted. It can be read on its own, or as a whisper of what's still to come—of hearts healing, legends stirring, and the promise that love can outlast even the dark.

Thank you for walking through the snow with me tonight. May your own Solstice bring warmth, wonder, and just a little bit of magic.

With love,
Alena

For everyone who knows legends are never just stories—
they're echoes of truth,
whispers of what came before,
and warnings of what might come again.

CONTENT WARNING

The Lantern's Shadow contains emotional themes of loss, mild peril, and sensual intimacy between consenting adults.

CHAPTER 1
MOONWATER FALLS

The air smelled of spice and frost, the kind of crisp that kissed her nose and painted her breath white. Saree pulled her scarf higher and slowed as the first notes of a fiddle wound through the bustling Solstice market. Lanterns swung from wooden posts overhead, their golden light blurring in the faint fall of snow. Somewhere nearby, a pot of mulled wine simmered, its sweet scent wrapping around her like a cocoon of festive joy.

Moonwater Falls looked like it belonged on a postcard—snug cabins pressed close along the main street, roofs heavy with snow, strings of garlands and fairy lights stretched between balconies. Laughter spilled from the taverns, boots crunched in the slush, and children's cheeks glowed red as they chased one another with snowballs. It was all too cheerful, too alive for the ache sitting behind Saree's ribs.

She should have stayed home. Or gone anywhere else for Solstice.

But anywhere else meant questions—from her mother, her cousins, her aunt with a pitying smile. *How's Jason? Are you two still living together? We were all expecting wedding news by now, dear...* And Saree couldn't stand to explain, not again, that Jason would no longer be coming to those family gatherings. The magic between them—gentle Jason with his gift for plants, and her, the unstable fire of an Empath—no longer worked. He wanted a family. She was not ready.

She'd thought a little time apart might dull the sharpness of it, but even now, walking through a market glowing with light and laughter, she could still feel the hollow where love had been.

Saree hadn't planned to stay the night. She'd only meant to walk through the markets, maybe catch a late train home. But as evening fell and the snow thickened, Moonwater Falls felt too magical to leave.

Saree stopped by a stall selling Solstice charms—small glass orbs filled with pressed pine needles and gold flakes. "They grant good luck," said the vendor, a kind-faced woman bundled in three layers of knit. "If you believe in it, of course."

Saree smiled faintly and bought one. "I'll take my chances." The orb was cool in her palm, smooth and perfect. She slipped it into her coat pocket and turned toward the heart of the market.

Warmth glowed everywhere she looked—from fire-places, from the crowd, from the simple joy of people who didn't need magic to feel connected. Maybe that's what hurt most. Her own gift had been both a blessing and a burden since childhood. Every brush of emotion, every flicker of thought too strong to stay contained. She could feel the collective happiness of Moonwater Falls pressing against her skin now, bright and dizzying.

She'd learned to keep it at arm's length, to breathe through it until the tide passed. But still, sometimes, she wished she could switch it off.

A burst of laughter made her glance toward the tavern terrace. A man and woman clinked glasses of spiced cider, cheeks flushed. A little girl waved a lantern shaped like a deer, its paper body glowing white. Saree's chest tightened. She'd forgotten how full Solstice nights could feel when she wasn't part of anyone's story.

She moved toward the fountain at the market's centre, silent in the winter but undoubtedly singing in the warmer months. A carved stag stood proudly in the snow, its eyes blind to the joy around it. Its antlers carried an intricate lantern, a symbol of the town's oldest legend that Saree learned about on her train here.

The Lantern Stag.

Every winter Solstice, the story went, the stag appeared to lost travellers and led them home through the snowfall. The golden glow of the lantern in its antlers showed the way. If your heart was pure, it might even grant you a wish. Saree smiled to herself. *A nice tale for tourists.* But something about the statue, the way the snow gathered around its hooves and the light haloed its head, tugged at her imagination. She'd grown up on legends like this, back before she'd realised how cruel the real world could be.

She turned away, tucking her hands into her coat pockets. Her heart's desire was too complicated even for herself, let alone a mythical creature.

"Saree?"

The voice was familiar enough to make her freeze.

She turned, heart skipping. Impossible. She travelled so far from Whitestone all the way to this tiny resort town by the Alps to make sure she escaped any familiar faces, and yet someone managed to bump into her even here. Levi, of all people. She was not in the mood for his banter and easy-going attitude, and definitely for his mind reading ability. She was here to rest, not strain herself even more with wards and shields. Levi seemed his usual carefree self, his coat open against the cold, dark curls catching stray snowflakes. She smiled despite herself. Maybe this encounter was meant to be. Maybe she wasn't supposed to be alone on this festive night, after all.

A mischievous glint danced in his eyes, the one that always spelled trouble during classes.

He grinned when he reached her, breath visible in the cold. "So. Saree the Empath."

She raised an eyebrow. "Levi the Mind-Reader. What brings you here?"

"Fate. Or mulled wine. Possibly both." He offered her one of the steaming paper cups he carried, the spicy scent curling between them. "You look like you could use this."

She hesitated, then took it, fingers brushing his for the briefest moment. "How'd you even spot me in this crowd?"

He shrugged. "You were brooding in high definition. Kind of hard to miss."

Saree snorted. "Thanks."

"You're welcome." He sipped his own drink, eyes scanning the market. "You here with someone?"

"No." She didn't elaborate.

Levi nodded, as if that explained everything. "Same. Just passing through, needed a change of scenery. Too many gloomy voices lately."

She knew what he meant. Mind-Readers like him never got much quiet. Even trained as he was, the constant buzz of thought could wear anyone down. Especially the kind of conflicting thoughts everyone had been having in Whitestone these past couple of months.

"I didn't think I'd see anyone from Whitestone here," she said.

He smiled sideways. "Guess the universe thought we needed company."

The two of them fell into step without meaning to, the market lights spilling in soft halos over their shoulders. Levi's energy was easy, filling the quiet without trying to fix it. Saree had forgotten how effortlessly he could do that. A term full of terrors, doubts and betrayals could mess anyone up, even the most seasoned teachers at Whitestone. And both of them were still only students.

They wandered past a row of stalls selling Solstice treats—sugared nuts, golden pastries filled with cinnamon and honey, gingerbread shaped like stars. The air shimmered with warmth and the distant strum of a guitar. Somewhere, a vendor called out for visitors to *"make a wish upon the Lantern!"*

"Don't tell me you're here chasing fairy tales," Saree said, taking another sip of her wine.

"Fairy tales?" Levi grinned. "Come on, this one's a local legend. The Lantern Stag appears to the pure of heart, grants one wish, and vanishes at dawn. Or something like that. How could I resist?"

Saree rolled her eyes, smiling despite herself. "So what would you wish for?"

He looked thoughtful for a heartbeat too long. "Peace and quiet," he said finally, half-joking, half not.

Her gaze softened. "Still can't block it all out, huh?"

Levi shrugged, kicking at the snow. "Some days are better than others. Whitestone taught me the tricks, but minds are loud things. And cities..." He exhaled, fog blooming from his lips. "They never shut up."

"I can relate," Saree said quietly. "Emotions don't sleep either."

He glanced at her, a trace of something deeper behind his grin. "Yeah, but at least you can feel the good ones too."

She smiled into her cup. "You'd be surprised how much harder that can make it."

They stopped at another stall, this one hung with hand-carved ornaments. The smell of pine resin drifted between them, grounding, real. Saree picked up a small deer carved from pale wood, its antlers etched with tiny stars.

"Lantern Stag?" Levi asked.

"Probably. Or just someone's attempt to make a quick coin."

He leaned closer, voice low. "Seriously though. Do you believe this legend has any grounds?"

"The Stag? No. It's just a story." She paused, her thumb tracing the deer's antlers. "Where I grew up, legends were like lullabies. Something to keep children hopeful in dark winters."

Levi smiled, his breath warm near her ear. "You sound like you miss it."

"I miss believing in it," she admitted.

For a moment, the music and laughter faded. Slow, beautiful snowflakes moved through the air, settling under their boots and immediately melting into slush. Saree hadn't noticed how close they stood until someone brushed past and their shoulders touched.

"Careful," Levi murmured. "You're drifting."

"Into sentimentality or your personal space?"

He chuckled. "A bit of both, I think."

Saree laughed, the sound small but genuine. "You're ridiculous."

"I've been called worse."

They walked again, shoulders occasionally bumping as the crowd jostled around them. The world had narrowed to golden light and cold air and the sound of their boots crunching in rhythm.

"Hey," Levi said after a while, "do you have plans for the night?"

Saree blinked. "Aside from pretending my personal issues don't exist? No."

"Then you're coming with me."

"Excuse me?"

He nodded down the street, toward where the lights of the market gave way to a distant lodge, its sign glowing *Moonwater Resort*. "It's got a fireplace, hot cider, and apparently one of the best Solstice views in town. You can brood in style."

"Brooding implies drama," she said, arching a brow. "I'm just... reflecting."

"Sure," he said easily. "Reflect at the resort, then."

Saree hesitated, but the warmth in his grin and the faint, unfamiliar spark in her chest made it hard to refuse. "Fine," she said. "But only because my feet are freezing."

CHAPTER 2
ONE ROOM AT THE INN

The Moonwater Resort stood at the very edge of town, perched between the last row of lamplit chalets and the dark sweep of the forest beyond. From the street, its windows glowed with a welcoming amber light. Garlands looped along the timber balcony, silver bells chiming softly in the wind. Smoke curled from the chimney, sweet with pine and something faintly spiced—mulled cider, perhaps. It was the sort of place Saree might have imagined in a storybook: warm, content, utterly untouched by the world's troubles.

She wasn't sure what she expected to feel when she stepped inside. But the wave of heat, the scent of burning cedar, and the soft crackle of firelight wrapped around her like an embrace.

Levi grinned, brushing snow from his coat as they crossed the lobby. "See? Told you it was worth the walk."

"You were pretty convincing, I'll give you that."

"Would you like dinner first or see if we can get a place for the night?" Levi asked.

Saree thought about her aching shoulders and the weight of the backpack that was starting to feel like a burden despite only containing the necessities.

"I didn't even think to book anything," she admitted, tugging her backpack higher on her shoulder. "I wasn't planning to stay."

"Good thing I'm an expert at charming receptionists," Levi said.

"Let's see if we can check in. I'd love to drop off my stuff and get my back a bit of rest."

A woman in her fifties with kind eyes and a Solstice brooch pinned to her vest looked up from her screen behind the reception desk. "Evening! Welcome to Moonwater Resort. Do you have a booking?"

Levi leaned an elbow on the counter, his easy smile sliding effortlessly into place. "Not yet, but we're hoping for a miracle."

The woman's expression softened. "Oh, I wish I could help, truly. But we're fully booked for the Solstice week."

Saree sighed, not surprised. "Figures."

"Maybe check again?" Levi said with mock optimism. "You never know. Might be a cancellation somewhere, or something like divine intervention, festive spirit..."

He slid a neatly folded banknote across the polished counter.

The receptionist hesitated, cheeks colouring. "Oh. Well, I suppose it can't hurt to double-check." Her fingers danced over the keyboard. A pause. Then her face brightened. "Actually, we've had a last-minute cancellation. One room left."

Levi smiled, victory soft and smug. "The Solstice spirits smile upon us."

Saree folded her arms. "They do, indeed."

"Pays off being resourceful," he said with a smug smile.

The receptionist handed him the keycard. "Room 207. Queen bed. Breakfast from seven until ten, buffet style."

Saree blinked. "I'm sorry, what kind of bed?"

"Queen."

Her gaze snapped to Levi. He, of course, was already smirking. "Guess we'll, ah, figure that out when we get there."

"Don't even start," Saree warned.

"Wouldn't dream of it," he said innocently, slipping the keycard into his pocket.

The receptionist's smile twitched, clearly trying not to laugh. "Enjoy your stay, you two."

***

Their room was on the second floor, overlooking the snow-draped forest. Saree paused in the doorway, the warm light spilling over her boots. The space was small but lovely—dark timber walls, a faux fireplace humming softly in the corner, and a bed so perfectly made it looked almost sinful to disturb. The air smelled faintly of pine resin, soap, and a hint of smoke from the fires below.

Levi stepped in beside her, brushing melting snow from his chestnut curls. They'd grown longer since last term at Whitestone, falling into loose waves that made him look boyish and entirely too charming. His brown eyes caught the firelight, full of mischief.

"I see you're not into spikes anymore," she said, tugging off her gloves. She dropped her backpack by the door.

"That's out of fashion." He ran a hand through the damp curls with a grin. "I'm growing them out now. You like?"

"It's... different." Saree loosened her scarf, letting her blond braids fall forward over her shoulders. His gaze flicked to them; she pretended not to notice.

Levi took one look at the bed and announced, "Dibs on the left side."

"You're not sleeping in the bed."

"You think I'm sleeping on the floor? On Solstice night?"

"You bribed your way into this situation."

"I negotiated."

Saree crossed her arms. "Then negotiate yourself a couch."

He laughed and flopped onto the edge of the mattress. "It's practically two beds. Look—neutral territory in the middle. No one crosses the pillow border."

"Uh-huh." She tried not to smile. "Do you snore?"

"Only when dreaming of being chased by ghost deer."

"Perfect," she muttered, dropping her pack by the dresser. "Then I'll need earplugs."

"Noted."

He leaned back on his elbows, still grinning, the firelight tracing the sharp lines of his face. Saree turned to the window to hide her laugh and steady her breathing. Outside, dusk had deepened into a rich indigo. The town glittered below them—garlands glowing gold, the market still alive with laughter. Beyond it, the forest rose like a wall of ink and snow, ancient and unknowable.

"Strange," Saree murmured. "The forest looks closer than before."

Levi frowned. "Maybe it's just the shadows."

She pulled her coat tighter. "We should go before it gets too late."

Levi sat up. "Dinner? I'm in."

"Explore, you goose. Dinner can wait. I'm not letting you waste a night in a place this beautiful."

His grin softened into something genuine. "You really think it's beautiful?"

"I think it's... peaceful." She hesitated, violet eyes catching his. "And I haven't had a lot of that lately."

He studied her for a moment, the teasing gone from his face. "Then it's settled," he said quietly. "We'll go find some peace to explore before we freeze to death."

On the way out, Levi paused by a small wooden stall near the inn's steps, its counter crowded with Solstice trinkets—tiny carved deer, hand-knit mittens, and lanterns painted gold.

"Hang on," he said, picking one up. Its frosted glass flickered with a soft, candlelike glow that pulsed faintly, almost as if breathing. Another setting on the switch produced a clean, bright light. "If we're wandering into the dark, we might as well do it in style."

Saree arched a brow. "Planning to summon the Lantern Stag yourself?"

He grinned. "I prefer to think of it as blending in with the locals. It's an actual lantern too, not just a gimmick."

The vendor handed him the lantern in exchange for a few coins. Levi lifted it, testing the light against the dusk. "See? Practical *and* festive."

Saree shook her head, smiling despite herself. "You're ridiculous."

"Ridiculously prepared," he corrected. "Lead the way, Empath."

***

They left the warmth of the resort behind, stepping into the crisp night air. Snowflakes drifted lazily, dusting their coats and hair. The town had transformed since sunset, growing softer, quieter. Strings of fairy lights framed every doorway, flickering gold and amber against the darkening sky. Children's laughter rippled from the frozen lake at the square's edge, where skaters drew shimmering loops beneath the lanterns. Blades whispered against the ice, the rhythm strangely hypnotic, as if the whole lake breathed with them. For a heartbeat, Saree could swear the reflections in the water moved on their own—lantern light bending like a pulse beneath the surface.

The smell of roasted chestnuts and woodsmoke lingered in the air. Somewhere, a group of carolers sang an old Solstice tune, their voices weaving through the night with the charm of winter. Saree's heart tightened unexpectedly. This was what happiness should look like. The simple kind. Laughter, warmth, the promise of safety.

"You're smiling," Levi said, his tone mock-conspiratorial.

"Am I?"

"Don't ruin it by denying it."

She looked at him, and for the first time since her break-up with Jason, she didn't deflect. "It feels like another life," she said softly. "Back at Whitestone, I forget the world still looks like this sometimes."

He nodded. "To be fair, what else would you expect from a school of magic? Whitestone's... intense."

"That's one word for it." She smiled faintly. "Between Whitestone and everything after... it's easy to forget there's more to life than work and survival."

"Then maybe you were meant to bump into me," Levi said lightly. "The universe's way of scheduling a break."

She chuckled, the sound surprising her. "Fine. But next time, I'm choosing where we end up."

"Deal. Fewer snowdrifts, more fireplaces."

"And better company?"

"Impossible improvement."

They stopped by a small bridge overlooking the frozen creek. Candlelit jars hung from its railings, each glowing faintly gold. Beneath them, coins glinted under the ice—the wishes from warmer months, waiting to be granted, safeguarded by the claim of winter until spring came again.

"Do you think people actually believe?" Saree asked.

"In what?"

"In... all of this. The wishes. The legends."

Levi leaned on the railing beside her. "You sound like you want to."

"I used to," she admitted. "When I was a kid, before I understood what power was. Before magic stopped being a wonder and became..."

"A burden," he finished for her.

She looked at him, surprised.

He smiled faintly. "You forget who you're talking to. I get it. I hear everything people think about their own power—how proud, how scared, how broken. It's a mess."

"You don't have to listen, you know."

"I don't mean to. It just leaks through." He shrugged. "I was lucky, though. The Nursery locked my magic when I was a baby. I didn't have to deal with the noise until puberty, when it came back naturally."

"That must've been nice."

He made a face. "You ever been thirteen and able to hear what everyone in your class thinks about you? Horrifying. Absolute trauma."

Saree laughed, the sound bubbling up before she could stop it. "Alright, fair point."

He looked pleased, the sound of her laughter clearly worth the confession. "What about you?"

"My magic didn't get locked," she said. "My parents didn't believe in the Nursery's methods and thought they could help me handle it. They meant well, but it was... a lot. I couldn't tell where their feelings ended and mine began. I cried for things that weren't mine to grieve."

Levi's expression softened. "That sounds awful."

"It was confusing." She smiled sadly. "Luckily, one of my old aunts had the same gift. She taught me to separate myself from others. It took years. Even now, sometimes, I slip."

"Guess that's why you're so good at understanding people."

"Or at least pretending to."

They stood there a moment, the silence between them not uncomfortable this time. Saree could feel warmth spreading through her chest. Not magic, not empathy. Just... connection.

Then Levi bumped her shoulder lightly. "You're thinking too hard."

"I'm thinking just enough."

He grinned. "Dangerous habit. Come on, Empath. We've got legends to chase."

"Levi—"

"Don't worry. I've got a good feeling about this."

"That's what people say before they do something stupid."

"Then it's a good thing we're brilliant."

Saree sighed, though the smile tugging at her lips betrayed her. "You're impossible."

"And yet here you are," he said, stepping back onto the path.

She followed him, snow crunching under their boots, laughter soft in the air.

As they walked, Saree glanced once more at the tree line. The forest loomed close now, its edges blurred by drifting snow. For just a heartbeat, the laughter and music from town seemed to fade, swallowed by a deeper, older silence.

The kind that listened back.

She blinked, and it was gone. The children's laughter returned, the bells chimed somewhere overhead, and Levi was grinning at her over his shoulder, asking if she was coming.

But the unease lingered, a whisper at the back of her mind. The sense of something vast and patient waiting just beyond the lights.

"Yeah," she said softly, tightening her scarf as she hurried to catch up. "I'm coming."

CHAPTER 3
THE DARE

The snow had quieted to a gentle hush by the time they left the bridge behind. The market lights faded into a blur of gold and red, their laughter softening into the rhythm of their boots crunching over snow. Saree didn't know where they were heading—only that the path felt right, the kind that led somewhere important even if she didn't yet know why.

Moonwater Falls was alive in its quiet way. Lanterns swayed in the wind, scattering flecks of light across frost-coated branches. The air was cold enough to nip at Saree's cheeks, but she welcomed it. The bite of it was grounding, real, something to anchor her in the here and now.

Levi walked beside her with his hands stuffed in his pockets, the easy slouch of someone who could never stay still too long. "You know," he said lightly, "I used to come here with my family when I was little. My mum loved this place. Said it looked like the inside of a snow globe."

"That's not wrong," Saree said, smiling. "It's almost too perfect."

"Exactly." His grin tilted. "Too perfect to be real. My mum used to bring me here, before everything got messy. Said this place existed halfway between magic and wishful thinking." His voice went quieter, softer. "Back then I just liked the hot chocolate." He shrugged, trying for lightness and missing it. "Now I get what she meant. Sometimes it's easier to believe in pretty lies than live in the truth."

Saree glanced around at the lights, the laughter, the delicate flurry of snowflakes tumbling like glitter under the streetlamps. "It does feel like a wish, doesn't it?"

Levi hummed agreement, and for a moment, silence stretched between them. Saree found herself grateful for it. The past few months had been noise: lessons, arguments, Jason's voice still lingering in her head when she didn't want it there. Here, there was peace.

But peace, she'd learned, was rarely just peace. It always left room for truth.

"I didn't expect to see anyone from Whitestone here," she said, breaking the quiet. "I came to be alone, actually."

Levi shot her a sidelong glance. "And yet, here I am. You're welcome."

She rolled her eyes, smiling despite herself. "That's not what I meant."

"I know. But I also know that sometimes being alone just means being tired."

Her steps slowed. "You read that off me?"

"No." He looked almost sheepish. "Guessed. I try not to pry anymore. It's a habit I'm still unlearning."

She hesitated, then said softly, "Thank you."

He nodded, gaze fixed ahead. "It's hard to turn it off. People's thoughts are like static. Even when you block one station, ten more tune in. Makes it hard to be close to anyone. Hard to know if what you feel is real, or just borrowed from someone else."

The raw honesty in his tone tugged something inside her. "That sounds lonely."

He smiled without humour. "It is. But you learn to live with it. Blaze says discipline takes time."

Saree laughed lightly. "He would."

Levi's grin returned, small but genuine. "He tried to train me in the very beginning, when he first came by our house to see if I was gifted enough to go to Whitestone. Back before I could block anyone out at all. He even let his own shields down to sharpen my focus and avoid distractions. I lasted three minutes before blurting out that he was worried about the traffic that was building up on his way back to the hotel and that he'd have to take a portal."

Saree snorted. "Oh no. You didn't."

"Did. He wasn't impressed. I think that's when he realised I was a lost cause and just handed me the school's enrolment form."

"He never gives up on his recruits," Saree said fondly. "He always checks in and then just looks disappointed until you feel so guilty you improve out of shame. So that the next time he stops by Whitestone, you actually make him proud."

Levi laughed, and it was a warm, easy sound. "That's accurate. He does that thing where he folds his arms and tilts his head? I swear he invented guilt with that look."

Saree smiled, shaking her head. "Maybe he just wants to keep us alive long enough to be worth his trouble."

"Probably," Levi agreed. "Though I think you were always one of his favourites."

She blinked. "What makes you say that?"

"The way he talks about you. Calm, reliable, controlled. The kind of student who listens." He gave her a teasing look. "Unlike me."

"I wasn't exactly perfect," she said. "But I did try. Empathy's... complicated. When I was little, I didn't know how to separate myself from everyone else. I'd absorb their pain without meaning to. Their sadness, their anger, their grief... I felt like being a sponge made of nerves."

Levi's expression softened. "That sounds awful."

"It was overwhelming. But with enough training, I was able to move ahead."

"That explains why you always seem so... steady," Levi said quietly. "Even when everything's falling apart."

Saree smiled faintly. "You've seen me steady. You haven't seen me cracked."

He looked at her for a moment, eyes unreadable. "Maybe I have. Just not in ways you realise."

Something in his tone made her chest tighten. She turned her face toward the snow to hide it. "You shouldn't read people like that."

"I didn't. Not this time."

Their breath mingled in the air between them, visible in little bursts of white. The wind shifted, carrying a faint Solstice melody from town that drifted and dissolved in the trees.

After a moment, Saree said quietly, "Jason used to hum that song."

Levi didn't reply right away. "He did?"

She nodded. "We were together for a long time. Everyone thought we'd end up married."

"What happened?"

Saree hesitated. "He wanted more than I could give. You know how he is. Quiet, grounded, easy-going. He wanted a family. Everyone else wanted it for us. But I just... don't feel this way yet. I want to travel, to explore, to have adventures. Not stay at home with babies. Maybe one day."

"Just not today." He finished for her.

She gave a weak laugh. "Exactly."

"Maybe he'd be the one staying home with babies while you go on adventures." Levi smirked, the glint of mischief lighting up in his eyes again.

Saree chuckled. "Maybe. But I wouldn't do this to him." She flicked her hand at a snow-covered pine, bringing down a miniature avalanche. "Parenting takes two. And I'm just not ready."

Levi didn't respond.

They fell into a companionable silence as the snow deepened, boots crunching softly in rhythm. The lights of Moonwater Falls shimmered behind them, golden and distant, while the forest ahead waited in shadow. A stray gust tugged loose a few strands from Saree's braids, brushing pale gold across her scarf.

Levi glanced over, a faint smile curving his mouth. "You always wear your hair like that?"

"Like what?"

"Two braids. Suits you," he said lightly, but there was curiosity beneath his teasing. "Is there a story behind it?"

Saree hesitated, eyes tracing the faint glow of lanterns behind them. "Where I'm from, single girls wear two braids. It's a custom, old as the hills. When a woman's ready to share her heart or her body with someone, she unbinds them. When she marries, she wears one."

His brows lifted. "So it's like a signal."

She nodded once. "If the man's paying attention."

"And if he isn't?"

"Then he's not worth unbinding them for," she said simply.

He chuckled under his breath, but his voice had gone softer. "Remind me to start paying attention, Empath."

Their eyes met, just long enough for the air to tighten between them, charged and fragile. Then Saree looked away, brushing snow from her coat.

"Come on," she said. "Before you get any more ideas."

"I've already got plenty," he murmured.

They walked on, their shoulders brushing now and then. The snow deepened, crunching underfoot like sugar. Frost painted the world in silver and white, and the moon hung low above the treetops, round and watchful.

Saree glanced at the sky. "It's beautiful tonight. No more clouds, just stars."

"Perfect for spotting mythical creatures," Levi said.

"Are you still on about that?"

"Of course. The Lantern Stag appears only on Solstice night, remember? Grants wishes, leads the lost home, all that legend stuff."

Saree smiled. "Seriously. You actually believe in that?"

He shrugged. "I believe in magic. Hell, I *have* magic. Who says stories aren't real?"

"They're not the same thing."

"Aren't they?" He turned to her, eyes bright. "Magic is what we do. Stories are what we hope for."

She considered that. "You sound like you've practiced that line."

"Maybe I have. It usually works better in taverns."

Saree laughed again, her breath clouding the air. "You're weird."

He leaned closer. "Possible. But admit this is more fun than moping in a hotel room or sitting in an overheated restaurant."

"You were the one desperate for dinner, Levi."

"Eh. Details."

They turned down a narrower trail that wound between cabins. The sounds of the town fell away until it was just the two of them, walking beneath the skeletal arms of snow-laden pines. Every sound was crisp: the crunch of their boots, the faint whisper of falling flakes, the occasional snap of a branch shedding its icy burden.

Saree slowed as they neared the forest's edge. The trees rose taller here, ancient and dark, their silhouettes inked against the star-bright sky. The mountains loomed beyond, dusted white, and somewhere high above, a lone owl called.

Levi stopped beside her, his face lit faintly blue by the moonlight. "Looks like the perfect place to find a ghost stag."

"Or freeze to death."

"Optimist."

"Realist," she countered. "The legend's a bedtime story. A way to make kids believe in magic."

He smiled, stepping closer until she could see the fine mist of his breath, the glint of humour in his eyes. "Then let's prove it."

She blinked. "You're serious."

"Completely."

"You don't even know where to look."

He nodded toward the trees. "That's the fun part."

"Levi—"

"Come on, Saree. We've both spent too long being sensible." His voice softened. "One night. One story. Let's see where it goes."

For a moment, she just stared at him—the curve of his smile, the spark of something reckless and alive in his eyes. Her heart beat too fast, too loud. Maybe it was the Solstice air, or the way the moonlight lightened his eyes, or simply that she was tired of carrying her pain alone.

"Fine," she said at last, voice low. "But if we get lost, I'm blaming you."

He grinned, triumphant. "Deal."

They stood together at the edge of the forest, stars burning cold and clear above them, the snow stretching pale and untouched ahead. Saree felt the hush settle over the world, deep and absolute.

"It's just a story," she whispered.

Levi reached for her hand, his touch warm through his glove. "Then let's prove it."

And together, they stepped into the waiting dark.

CHAPTER 4
INTO THE STILLNESS

The forest waited for them in its breathless hush. Snow muffled the world until even their footsteps sounded like whispers swallowed by the night. The trail wound beneath the black lace of pine branches, each heavy with white, bending under winter's still hand. The air smelled of ice and bark and something faintly sweet—the clean scent of deep cold, untouched and ancient.

Saree's breath came out in pale clouds, steady but quick. The quiet pressed against her ears, so complete it almost rang. She'd thought she knew silence from the library halls of Whitestone, or the tranquil meditation rooms where she learned control over her magic, but this was different. This silence was alive. Listening.

Beside her, Levi's lantern from the resort's gift shop swung in the dark, its single ray piercing the night. "You ever think about them?" he asked suddenly.

"Who?"

"Ayla and Blaze. The destined pair."

Saree blinked, surprised by the shift from wonder to sorrow. "Sometimes," she admitted. "Hard not to. Everyone at Whitestone talked about them after she... after what happened."

Levi nodded. "I keep wondering how that works—being destined. Like, what does it *feel* like to know someone is meant to be with you forever?"

Saree smiled faintly. "From what I've heard, it's overwhelming, at least in the beginning. Magical. Terrifying, probably. You feel each other's pain, each other's emotions. There's no privacy between the destined."

Levi made a face. "Sounds exhausting."

"Sounds romantic," she countered softly. "When it works."

"And when it doesn't?"

She hesitated, then said, "Then it's hell. You can't undo it. You can't just stop loving them, even if you try."

Levi gave a small laugh. "Guess I'll stick to mortal heartbreak, then."

She glanced at him. "You say that like you've had your share."

"Maybe." He gave her a sidelong smile. "Admit it though. You had a thing for Blaze too, like all the other girls."

Saree laughed, the sound echoing gently off the trees. "I respected him. He's an excellent teacher."

"Come on. He's got that whole 'I've-seen-too-much' tragic hero vibe."

She snorted. "If you'd seen what he's seen, you might have gotten it, too."

"Fair," Levi said, grinning. "Still. Can't blame people for noticing."

They walked in companionable silence for a few minutes, their lantern swaying between the trees. Then Levi said, more quietly, "What do you think will happen to him now that she's gone?"

Saree's step faltered. "You mean Ayla?"

He nodded.

"Well..." She exhaled, watching her breath drift into the dark. "He'll suffer. A lot. I heard that if one of the destined dies, the other doesn't just grieve. It's like losing half of your soul. But Blaze... he's strong. He still shows up to lessons, still recruits for Whitestone. You can tell it's weighing on him, though. He looks... hollow."

Levi's voice softened. "Do you think she's really gone?"

"We all saw her body. The Healers pronounced her dead," Saree said after a pause. "There's no way she could have survived."

"Still." He scuffed at the snow with his boot. "I'd think Blaze would vanish after that. Go full hermit in the mountains or drink himself blind. Instead, he's still out there. Doing his job like nothing happened. But when I try to read him... nothing. His thoughts are a fortress. Completely sealed, like usual. Not the shattered mess of someone who just lost their destined mate."

"Blaze has always been disciplined," she murmured. "Maybe that's what keeps him alive. Duty."

"Or denial."

Saree gave him a long look. "Maybe both."

Levi smiled faintly, but it didn't reach his eyes. "You know, I keep thinking... what if she isn't dead?"

Saree frowned. "What do you mean?"

"What if she's *somewhere else*? I don't know, like in the Mist, maybe. Not gone, just... trapped. The legends say Mistwalkers never really die, right?"

She hesitated, her heartbeat loud in the quiet. "They say that. That their souls remain in the Mist instead of crossing to the afterlife. But if that were true—"

She stopped. The words caught in her throat.

The forest had gone utterly still.

Levi noticed it too. His steps slowed, his gaze sweeping the shadows between the trees.

"Hear that?"

Saree listened. No rustle of branches, no scurry of small animals, not even the sigh of wind through the pines. Just silence.

"I don't feel anything," she whispered.

"What do you mean?"

"There's no life here. No emotion. Usually, there's a hum, even faint—animals, people far off, the residue of being alive. Here, there's nothing. It's like..." She swallowed. "Like the world's holding its breath."

Levi turned slowly in a circle, lantern raised. The light spilled over the snow and skeletal trees, illuminating a world that looked carved from ice.

"Maybe it's just the cold," he offered, though his tone lacked conviction.

Saree shook her head. "No. This isn't natural."

He looked back at her, brow furrowed. "We can turn around if you want."

She hesitated. "No. Not yet."

He smiled a little. "Brave."

"Foolish."

"Same thing sometimes."

She wanted to laugh, but her chest felt too tight. They walked a few more steps, their lantern's glow shrinking against the endless white. Saree felt the quiet press harder now, dense and suffocating. She reached out instinctively with her gift, brushing her awareness against the world, and winced.

It was like touching ice. Cold, empty, unfeeling.

"Levi..."

He turned, and for a heartbeat, the light caught his face—the fine mist of his breath, the faint line between his brows. "Yeah?"

"I don't think we're alone."

He stilled. "You sense something?"

"I sense *nothing*."

"That's worse," he muttered.

Their eyes met, and for the first time that night, Saree saw the faint edge of fear flicker through his confidence. It made her strangely bold. "You don't have to hide it. You feel it too."

He didn't deny it. "When I'm near you, the noise disappears. Normally I can hear people's thoughts from miles off. A blur, a murmur, something. But around you..." He exhaled. "It's quiet. Too quiet. I thought it was peace. Now I'm not so sure."

Her chest tightened. "Maybe it's both."

They stood there for a moment, close enough to see the reflection of the lantern in each other's eyes. Somehow, the sky grew darker, covered by heavy clouds that hadn't been there minutes ago. The snow started falling around them, soft and endless, whispering against their coats. Saree wanted to reach out, to ground herself with touch, to prove he was still real in this silent world, but before she could, something flickered at the edge of her vision.

"Levi," she said sharply. "Look."

A trail of broad, deep impressions curved ahead through the snow.

He crouched, lantern low. "Tracks."

Saree joined him, heart hammering. "Too big for deer."

"Too heavy," Levi agreed. He took off his gloves and brushed the nearest print. "Saree. It's warm."

She blinked. "That's not possible."

"Touch it."

She did. And flinched. The snow should have been ice-cold, but the hollow where something massive had stepped pulsed faintly with warmth. Almost like the earth itself still remembered the weight of its passage.

"It's like it just happened," she murmured.

Levi stood slowly, scanning the shadows ahead. The tracks glowed faintly with an echo of the light, as if silver ink was shifting beneath the surface.

Saree's breath hitched. "That's not—"

"Natural?" he finished. "No."

She closed her eyes for a moment, reaching out again with her gift. The emptiness was still there, but beneath it was something else. A hunger. Cold and endless. It scraped against her senses, vast and hollow, like staring into a pit that had no bottom.

Her eyes flew open. "Something's wrong."

Levi's hand found her arm. "What do you feel?"

"Not emotion. Not life. Just... absence."

He swallowed hard. "And I'm hearing static. Like white noise in my head. It's everywhere. I can't focus."

Saree glanced down at the glowing tracks, the faint shimmer that distorted the air above them like heat haze. "Maybe we should go back."

Levi hesitated. "We're so close."

"To what?" she asked.

He smiled faintly, though his eyes were tense. "To finding out if legends have teeth."

"Levi—"

"Come on. Maybe this is how it's supposed to feel."

Saree wanted to protest, to drag him back toward the lights of Moonwater Falls. But her curiosity, destiny, or perhaps the pull of the Solstice itself kept her rooted.

She nodded once. "Fine. But if we die, I'm haunting you."

He grinned, a flicker of mischief in the dread. "Worth it."

They followed the tracks.

The deeper they went, the heavier the snow fell. It blurred the trees into shadows, smudging the line between reality and dream. Saree kept her eyes on the faint glow ahead, on the rhythm of their steps, on the warmth of Levi's presence beside her. The static in the air seemed to hum now, faint but insistent, threading through her nerves like a warning.

The wind died entirely. The forest held its breath once more.

And far ahead, through the snowfall, a single light flickered—gold, pale, and beckoning.

Levi exhaled a slow, trembling laugh. "Well. Guess we found our legend."

Saree's heart stuttered. "Or it found us."

CHAPTER 5
THE LANTERN STAG

The tracks led them deeper until the forest thinned.

The trees opened suddenly, as though drawn back by unseen hands, revealing a glade washed in silver moonlight. The sky looked deep and dark, not a cloud in sight. The snow here looked untouched, smooth and glimmering faintly, as if the stars had fallen and melted into it. Saree stopped just beyond the last tree, breath caught in her throat.

Levi lifted the lantern, but its golden glow was weak against the vast light of the moon. "You feel that?" he whispered.

She nodded. Her skin tingled. The air was sharp and electric, humming with energy that felt older than the world. She could taste metal on her tongue—ozone, frost, and something else, something that prickled behind her eyes.

At the far side of the clearing, mist rose from the snow in thin curls. Not the fog of warmth meeting cold, but tendrils of luminous haze that pulsed with faint blue light through the grey. They drifted, coiling like breath from invisible lungs.

And then, between those ribbons of light, a shape began to form.

Levi froze. "Holy hell."

It stepped forward slowly, hooves pressing deep into the glowing snow. A creature so beautiful Saree's heart stuttered just to look at it.

The Lantern Stag.

Its coat shimmered like the night sky itself—black velvet dusted with stars that flickered when it moved. Its antlers stretched high and impossibly wide, each tine aglow with spectral light. And hanging between them, swaying from a fine chain of silver, was a lantern.

The light inside burned faint and gold, soft and gentle, spilling across the snow like melted dawn.

Saree's breath trembled out. "It's real."

Levi only nodded, his mouth parted in awe. "That's... that's impossible."

"It's beautiful," she whispered.

For a moment, they both forgot the cold, the fear, everything. They just stood and watched, caught between wonder and disbelief. The Stag moved with slow, deliberate grace, not like an animal, but like something divine. It lowered its head to the snow and pawed delicately, breath misting like incense.

Levi spoke first, his voice barely a murmur. "Here it is. The Stag of legend that carries a lantern of eternal light. The spirit to guide the lost souls home through the winter storms."

Saree nodded. "Or to grant a single wish to the pure of heart."

He glanced sideways at her, a half-smile flickering through his awe. "Think we qualify?"

She might've smiled back, but something in her chest twisted when she sensed a wrongness beneath the beauty. The air felt too cold now, too heavy. Each breath scraped her lungs with ice.

The Stag raised its head.

The lantern flickered.

Once, twice—then the light changed.

The gold dissolved into a deep, searing blue.

Levi blinked. "That's—"

"Wrong," Saree whispered.

The blue light spread like ink through the clearing, painting the snow in shades of ghostly cerulean. The glow reflected in the Stag's eyes, and for the first time, Saree realised there was nothing inside them.

No depth. No life.

Just hollow darkness.

The beauty of it shattered. She saw now the way its body flickered, edges trembling like smoke. The starlight that seemed to shimmer through its hide wasn't light at all—it was movement. Tendrils of the same pale mist curling along its limbs, threading through fur and flesh like veins.

"Is this what the Mist looks like?" Levi breathed.

"I think so." Her voice was barely sound.

"Then something's wrong."

The Stag stepped forward, the snow crunching under its hooves with a sound that didn't belong to this world. Too wet. Too deep. Saree caught the faint smell of rot beneath the frost. The air around them thickened, humming with power that pressed against her chest.

"Levi," she whispered, "don't move."

"I'm not moving."

The Stag's lantern pulsed once, twice, and the air rippled outward in blue waves. The temperature dropped so fast Saree's breath froze white and sharp. Every nerve screamed *run*, but her legs wouldn't obey.

Levi's hand brushed hers, fingers trembling. "It's looking at us."

The creature's hollow gaze pinned them both. It lowered its head. The lantern swayed between its antlers, its blinding blue light a command to follow. *Stay still. Stay breathing. Stay alive.*

The snow at its hooves began to stir.

The ground shivered. Saree stumbled back. From the snow, thin, translucent silhouettes began clawing their way up from the frozen earth. They weren't solid, not quite real, but she could *feel* them: the echo of fear, grief, despair.

"Levi—"

"I see them." His voice shook.

The shadows multiplied, each one faceless, flickering, whispering. Their mouths didn't move, but the air was full of sound now: a chorus of broken murmurs, words she couldn't understand. The cold pressed against her skin like a living thing.

"What is this?" she gasped.

Levi's eyes were wide, unfocused. "Static," he whispered. "In my head. Too many voices—"

"Don't listen!"

"I can't block them out!"

Saree grabbed his arm. "Levi! Focus on me!"

He blinked, breathing hard. "Right. Right."

The shadows began to close in. The Stag lifted its head again, the lantern swinging, and the blue light grew stronger—feeding them, calling them. The glade pulsed like a living heart.

"Run," Saree whispered.

Levi didn't argue.

They turned and bolted through the snow. Branches lashed at their coats, snow burst under their feet. Saree's lungs burned with cold, her heart thundering in her ears. Behind them, she could hear the *thud* of hooves—impossibly heavy, impossibly fast.

"Left!" Levi shouted.

They veered off the trail, crashing through a thicket. Saree risked a glance back to see the Stag's light cut through the trees like a blade, illuminating the flickering shadows that followed in its wake. The air shimmered with frost and smoke.

"Keep going!" she gasped.

They stumbled over a fallen log, nearly falling. Levi caught her by the wrist, yanking her upright, and they kept running. The snow grew deeper, their steps slower. The light followed, relentless.

"Levi!" she cried. "We're not fast enough!"

He spun, raising his hand. A ball of pure white appeared over it in seconds. Saree stopped beside him, summoning her own magic. It answered eagerly as always, brilliant white flame dancing on her fingertips, ready for her command.

"Together," Levi muttered.

Their hands twisted, growing the light in their palms larger, shaping it like weapons. Levi's, a bow and glowing arrows. Saree's, a set of throwing knives.

There was no time to marvel at each other's choices. Both readied themselves for the wall of approaching mist, and the second the menacing silhouette was within range, they fired their weapons.

Nothing happened. The shadow didn't stop. It absorbed the power as if it was nothing but a gust of wind, and continued its onslaught.

"No good," Levi panted. "Our magic is useless."

"Back to plan A then. Go!"

Saree felt panic rise as she ran again. Her empathy reached out instinctively, brushing against the approaching storm—and recoiled. The emptiness there wasn't void; it was hunger. A bottomless craving for warmth, for emotion, for *life*.

The Stag wasn't bringing souls home. It was devouring them.

"Levi," she gasped, "it's feeding on us."

They stumbled into a narrow clearing, moonlight glinting off a half-frozen stream. Saree's chest ached, her breath ragged. The blue glow was closing in, shadows flickering at the edges of her vision.

"We can't outrun it," Levi said, voice hoarse.

"Then we don't."

He turned to her, eyes wild. "What?"

"I can try something else."

"Saree—"

"Trust me!"

He hesitated only a second before nodding. "Always."

Saree closed her eyes and reached inward, deeper than she ever had before. Her gift had always been about *feeling* others, absorbing their pain, their fear, their sorrow. It had never been meant to harm. But maybe, she thought, it didn't have to.

If she could *take* pain, maybe she could *give* peace.

She exhaled slowly, steadying herself. The shadows drew closer, whispering in voices that weren't human. She felt Levi's presence beside her, solid, trembling but steadfast.

"Whatever you're doing," he said quietly, "do it fast."

Saree opened her heart. She thought of warmth, of the laughter by the Solstice market, of her aunt's gentle hands, of the simple comfort of being known and not judged. She thought of the moment Levi had made her laugh, and the quiet that followed. She let those feelings flood through her.

Then she *pushed*.

The surge that left her was unlike anything she'd ever felt—a wave of emotion, bright and golden, bursting out from her chest. It rippled through the clearing like sunlight under ice.

The shadows screamed.

Where the light touched them, they faltered, wavering like smoke in the wind. The Stag's blue lantern flared violently, but the glow dimmed under her radiance. The mist recoiled, shuddering, retreating as if burned.

Levi caught her as she stumbled, eyes wide. "Saree! You did it—"

"Not for long," she gasped. Her head spun. Every ounce of strength poured out of her like sand through an hourglass. The shadows began to gather again at the edge of her light, twitching, reforming.

Levi grabbed her shoulders. "Then we move now!"

She nodded weakly. Together they turned and ran again, crashing through the snow as the glade erupted behind them in light and shadow, the Stag's roar echoing through the trees.

The forest blurred into streaks of white and black. Saree's legs felt like lead, her vision a whirl of motion and pain. She clung to Levi's sleeve, letting him guide her through the twisting paths. The sounds of hooves, whispers, the creak of ice grew fainter behind them.

They didn't stop until they saw the faint orange glow of the town's lanterns through the trees. Saree nearly sobbed with relief.

"Almost there," Levi breathed. "Just a little further."

They broke from the treeline, stumbling onto the packed snow road. The laughter and music of the festival reached them. Normal life, still untouched by what they'd seen.

Saree turned once more toward the forest. The blue light flickered far back between the trees, faint and fading. For a heartbeat, she thought she saw the Stag's silhouette—tall, regal, watching. Then it was gone, swallowed by shadow.

Levi bent over, hands on his knees, breath ragged. "I'm officially retiring from ghost hunting," he wheezed.

Saree tried to laugh, but her voice came out thin. "Seconded."

They stood there, catching their breath, the chill finally settling into their bones. Saree's heart still pounded, but beneath the fear was a strange calm. A knowing.

She'd faced something from the Mist and lived.

Levi straightened, meeting her gaze. "You did it."

"I tried," she said softly. "I think I just confused it long enough for us to run."

"Whatever you did, it worked."

She managed a small smile. "Guess empathy isn't useless after all."

He smiled back, but there was something unspoken in his eyes—admiration, maybe more. The lantern light from the town's festive streets reflected in the snow ahead of them, soft and golden.

"Come on," he said finally. "Before I freeze solid and you have to carry me."

Saree laughed weakly. "You're impossible."

"And you like that about me."

"Maybe."

Together they walked back toward the warmth of Moonwater Falls. The music grew louder, the lights brighter. Saree glanced over her shoulder one last time.

The forest stood silent again, its secrets buried beneath the snow. But just before she looked away, she thought she saw a flicker of blue deep within the shadows. A faint pulse, like a lantern's glow waiting to be rekindled.

Her heart skipped.

"Let's go," Levi said softly, guiding her forward.

And though the night behind them fell quiet once more, Saree couldn't shake the feeling that something ancient and hungry had followed them home.

CHAPTER 6
THE SOLSTICE NIGHT

They didn't speak much as they trudged back down the trail. The sky stretched wide and clear above, stars glittering sharp and cold. Their boots crunched in rhythm, and the silence between them felt less like distance and more like shared relief.

When the golden lanterns of Moonwater Resort finally came into view, Levi drew a sharp breath and muttered, "Ah."

"Yes," Saree agreed softly, lips twitching despite her exhaustion. "That."

They both stopped and stared at each other, realisation striking at the same time. One bed. Of course. Saree pressed her mittened hand over her mouth, but laughter bubbled out anyway. Levi followed, shaking his head, eyes brighter than she'd seen them all night.

"Let's get cleaned up first," he said when they caught their breath again.

Inside, the resort lobby glowed with festive lights. A wreath of evergreen and silver ribbon hung over the reception desk. The cheerful clerk in a red scarf wished them a happy Solstice.

"And to you," Levi replied easily, fumbling for the key-card. "Though, if you've got any lanterns in the back, might I suggest... don't make your wish."

Saree coughed to cover her laugh. "Mulled wine's safer," she added, managing to keep her voice steady. "Trust us."

The clerk blinked, then chuckled, clearly used to tipsy guests saying strange things on Solstice Eve.

The room felt like the most welcoming place on the planet. The heat from the faux fireplace was almost stifling after the long walk, wrapping Saree in a haze of safety and comfort.

She sat on the edge of the bed for a moment, pulling off her boots, letting the adrenaline finally ebb. They were alive. They'd faced something no Mage had ever spoken of, and lived.

"I'll take the first shower," Levi said, still a little too casual, but his eyes lingered on her as if making sure she was really all right.

"Go," Saree murmured, gesturing him away.

When the bathroom door shut, she lay back on the quilt, staring at the low-beamed ceiling. The night replayed in fragments—the stag's hollow eyes, the cold emptiness of the shadows, the way Levi's presence helped her keep her focus. She shivered, but it wasn't all fear.

Steam curled from under the bathroom door. When Levi re-emerged, his dark hair damp and curling at the ends, he'd changed into a simple t-shirt and sleep pants. Saree sat up quickly, tugging her bag toward her as though the movement explained her flushed cheeks.

"Your turn," he said gently.

She gathered her clothes, bundled her braids up with a hair clip to keep them from getting wet and disappeared into the bathroom. Hot water hit her skin, and for the first time since they'd fled the glade, she let herself breathe. The warmth eased the ache from her muscles, the steam softening the sharp edges of fear. When she closed her eyes, the stag's hollow gaze flashed behind her lids—the flicker of blue light, the hunger that wasn't just seen but felt. It had reached for her like a thought.

She pressed a hand over her heart. *No. It's over, at least for now.*

For a few minutes, she let herself absorb the warmth of the running water before turning off the shower. Saree wrapped herself in a towel, steam ghosting around her skin. When she stepped back into the room, the scent of cedar and something delicious greeted her. Levi had changed into a soft black shirt, sleeves rolled up, his damp curls falling boyishly over his forehead. He sat by the small table near the window, a tray set between two mugs.

"I might have raided the kitchen before they locked up," he said, lifting the lid from a small copper pot. "Ahh, the delightful winter stew. Veal, turnip, herbs, a splash of red wine for good measure. Just what the doctor ordered on a frosty night like this."

Steam curled into the air, savoury and sweet at once. Saree sat opposite him, and he poured steaming portions into shallow bowls. The smell was intoxicating—thyme, cloves, and slow-cooked meat mingled with the faint sweetness of wine. Saree took a spoonful, the warmth melting the chill from her bones.

"This is incredible," she said, surprised at the husky note in her own voice.

"Told you I was resourceful," he said. "To surviving fairy-tale disasters."

She smiled faintly, raising her mug. "And to making it back before the snow buried us."

They ate in a companionable quiet. Small portions to take the edge off the hunger. Outside, snow sifted through the night, flakes glinting in the lamplight beyond the glass. The warmth of the fire seeped through her limbs, softening the last of her tension.

When she looked up, Levi was watching her. "What?" she asked, self-conscious.

He shrugged. "You look different tonight."

She tried for levity. "Different as in exhausted and half-frozen?"

"As in real," he said softly.

That startled her more than she wanted to admit. For a moment she couldn't look at him; the air between them felt fragile, delicate as spun glass.

"What do you think it was?" he asked quietly.

She swallowed, her throat tightening. "I don't know. I don't think it was supposed to exist. Not like that."

Levi nodded slowly. "When you... reached out with your gift, I thought you'd vanish. You were glowing. Like the air around you couldn't decide whether to hold you or let you go."

Saree looked down at her hands. "I didn't know I could do that. Give instead of take. I just... reacted."

"You saved us."

"I don't know if I did." Her voice wavered. "Maybe it let us go."

He leaned closer, his tone gentler now. "You did something extraordinary, Saree. Don't take that from yourself."

The quiet settled deeper, charged now, full of things unsaid.

"It's dangerous," she whispered. "Letting someone close when you know they can hurt you."

"I know," he said, voice rough. "But tonight... I don't care."

Her heart stuttered. She wanted to tell him no, that it wasn't fair, that they were only here because of chance and fear and snow. But she was tired of being careful.

His eyes were so dark they caught the reflection of the lamp like molten amber. For a long time, neither of them spoke.

Levi stretched his legs out on the bed, the mug of chocolate balanced in his hand. "This really is a tricky situation," he murmured, half to himself. Then, with a faint smile: "You know, back home they say that you'll spend the whole year the way you spend your Solstice night."

Saree groaned softly. "Oh gods, please don't tell me we're facing a whole year full of terrifying Mist creatures and risking our lives running away from things we don't understand." Her voice was light, teasing, but the words clung to her ribs, heavier than she meant them. She pushed the thought away. That was enough for one night.

Levi's smile faltered, something softer slipping in. "Hope not," he said quietly. His thumb traced the curve of the mug. "I was thinking more about spending it with you."

Her chest tightened. The words hovered between them, tender and dangerous all at once. "This was one night, Levi," she reminded him, her tone gentler than she expected. "And we are very different people."

"Of course." His answer came too quickly, too eager to smooth over the fragile moment. "I didn't mean rushing into anything."

Her eyes lingered on his, catching the truth hidden beneath his protest. She let herself breathe into the stillness.

"We can just have this night to ourselves," she said, her voice quiet but steady. "After all we've been through."

His lips curved in a small, tired smile. "Just for tonight."

The words loosened something in her. The air shifted, less weighted by fear, more by awareness. The decadent scent of chocolate hung sweet and heavy between them, mixing with the sharp, clean cedar of his shampoo. The warmth of the fire display threw golden light across his face, softening the angles of his jaw, catching in the strands of his hair that refused to dry.

She set her mug aside. Her fingers, stiff from holding the ceramic, drifted to her braids. Unhurried, she began to undo them, her hands trembling only slightly. Levi's gaze flicked to her hands, then back to her face, hungry but reverent. She caught every detail: the way his breath hitched, the faint tremor of his throat when he swallowed, the way he gripped his mug too tightly before setting it aside as though he couldn't trust his hands. His chest rose and fell faster than before, and she realized she could hear it like the uneven rhythm of his breathing against the hush of the room.

Saree's pulse quickened, not just with anticipation but with something more fragile, more human: a need to be close, to anchor herself in warmth and touch after a night that had nearly broken her. Her skin prickled as she slipped her outer layers aside, acutely aware of his eyes on her, the weight of his longing written in every stolen glance.

She told herself she was only looking, only memorising, but the truth was she was just as hungry as he was. Hungry for the safety of another's arms. For the promise of rest in someone else's heartbeat. For something beautiful to cling to in a world that was falling apart.

Saree's fingers slipped free the last braid, her hair tumbling loose around her shoulders. For a moment, she felt bare in a way she hadn't expected, more revealing than skin alone. Levi's eyes softened, reverence threaded with want, as though he understood the weight of what she'd just given him.

The silence stretched, charged and waiting.

He shifted on the bed, and when his hand reached toward her, he hesitated just a breath before brushing his fingers against hers. The touch was simple, but the heat of it startled her, a spark racing up her arm.

"You're trembling," he whispered.

"So are you," she answered, and her lips curved before she could stop them.

He laughed shakily, then tugged her closer. The bed dipped under her weight as she joined him, their knees brushing. Saree could feel the warmth radiating from his skin, seeping into her, making her shiver despite the heat of the room.

Levi raised a hand, pausing again, as though giving her space to turn away. When she didn't, his fingers threaded carefully into her hair. She inhaled sharply at the sensation—the cedar lingering on his skin, the featherlight pressure of his touch against her scalp.

Her heart beat too fast. "Levi…"

"Just for tonight," he reminded her, his voice low and steady, though she could feel the tremor running through him.

Before she could answer, he leaned closer. His forehead rested against hers, breath mingling with hers in the narrow space between them. Saree closed her eyes, overwhelmed by the nearness, the way the whole world seemed to fall away until there was only this moment, only him.

His lips brushed hers—hesitant, questioning. Saree answered by leaning in, letting the kiss deepen, slow but sure. His hand slipped from her hair to cradle her cheek, thumb grazing the corner of her mouth.

The kiss grew hungrier, still unhurried but pulsing with a need that had been building all night. Saree's fingers curled into his shirt, pulling him closer, wanting the solid reassurance of his body against hers. He responded with a quiet sound, half-moan, half-exhale, the sound of someone who had been holding back far too long.

When they broke apart, it was only to breathe. Their foreheads touched again, their breaths uneven. Saree's pulse thrummed in her throat, dizzying. She looked at his flushed cheeks, his wide, unguarded eyes, and she felt her chest ache with something fierce and tender all at once.

"You're so beautiful," Levi whispered, his fingers brushing her cheek.

He drew her down into the bed, the both of them tangled in blankets, their bodies pressed together, exploring the edges of touch without rushing past them. The scent of cedar and chocolate wrapped around her, the heat of his skin a balm against the cold etched into her bones.

She arched into him, her body answering before her mind could catch up. His hands slid over her curves, reverent but hungry, lingering at her waist as though memorizing every line of her. Saree tugged at his shirt until he pulled it off entirely, and the sight of him above her made her breath hitch.

The firelight flickered across his skin, painting him in gold and shadow, his chest rising and falling too fast. His eyes burned when they met hers, and for a heartbeat, neither of them moved, caught between restraint and abandon.

Then Saree reached up, guiding him back down to her, and his restraint shattered. His mouth claimed hers, their kiss deepening into something wild and consuming. She felt his hands slide beneath the hem of her top, fingertips brushing over bare skin, and every touch left trails of fire.

Her own breaths came ragged, broken between kisses, and when she whispered his name it sounded like a plea. Levi answered by pressing his forehead to hers, his body trembling as though it took everything in him not to lose control.

His mouth claimed hers again, harder this time, stealing what little breath she had left. Saree clung to him, fingers splayed against the heat of his bare back, feeling every line of muscle flex beneath her touch. The kiss was nothing gentle now—it was wild, hungry, a storm neither of them could hold back any longer.

He kissed like he was drowning, like she was the only thing keeping him alive, and it tore her wide open. Her pulse thundered in her ears, matching the frantic rhythm of his heart. When his hand slid beneath her top and skimmed over her ribs, up the curve of her side, she gasped into his mouth, arching helplessly into the contact.

Her own hands were restless, tugging at him, exploring the breadth of his shoulders, the firm line of his chest. She wanted to feel all of him, memorize the warmth and strength, before reason or morning light could steal this away. Levi shuddered under her touch, his breath ragged against her lips.

"Gods, Saree..." His voice cracked as though the words hurt to say. "Tell me to stop, and I'll stop."

She shook her head fiercely, pulling him down again. "Don't you dare stop."

The sound he made was half groan, half surrender. He kissed her until her lips tingled, until she was dizzy from lack of air, and still it wasn't enough. His hand swept down her waist, lingering at her hip, before sliding lower to draw her against him fully. Saree's breath caught—heat, pressure, the undeniable proof of his desire—and it sent fire shooting through her veins.

She had never felt so alive, so desperately wanted.

"Just tonight," he rasped again, though his body betrayed him, clinging as though he'd never let go.

Saree pulled him closer, lips brushing his ear. "Then let's make tonight enough to last a lifetime."

The rest was heat and firelight, tangled limbs and desperate whispers, as the storm finally broke and carried them both away.

CHAPTER 7
WHAT THE FOREST KEPT

The room had gone quiet but for the hum of the heater and the faint hiss of snow against the windowpane. Saree stirred, restless beneath the heavy quilt, warmth wrapping her body yet unable to shake the pull of something just beyond the glass. Slowly, she eased herself up, bare feet meeting the plush rug with a muffled sigh of fabric. The scent of cedar still clung to her skin, threaded with the ghost of chocolate on her tongue.

She padded to the window and opened the curtains, her fingertips brushing the cold sill. Outside, the world was hushed in silver. Frost glittered like shards of glass across the branches. Snow lay in thick, unbroken swathes, pure as untouched canvas. And between the shadows of the trees there was light.

A faint glimmer. Not golden, like lanterns strung along the village streets. Not warm. This light pulsed cold and blue, eerie as a wound in the night. For one breathless moment she thought it was a trick of her tired eyes, some echo of memory. The glow swelled faintly, then dimmed, as if something out there drew breath. Watching. Waiting.

Her stomach tightened. She pressed closer to the glass, holding her breath as though it might hear her. Was it real, or was she dreaming on her feet?

Arms slipped around her waist, solid and warm, the familiar cedar-scent rising off damp skin. Levi rested his chin on her shoulder, silent. His heartbeat pressed steady against her back, a counterpoint to the thrum of that impossible light. He didn't ask what she saw. He didn't need to.

For a while they just stood there, watching the snow-silvered forest. The weight of silence carried more truth than words. They both knew it—whatever they had glimpsed tonight in the glade had not been left behind. It lingered. Waiting.

The fire display flickered low, casting amber glow across their entwined shadows. Saree let herself lean into his warmth, the shiver running down her spine less from cold than from knowing. She didn't want to name it. Not now.

Her lips curved faintly, the words a whisper caught in the frost on the window: "Happy Solstice, Levi."

He tightened his hold, his voice low, roughened with something unspoken. "Thank you... for tonight."

Snow drifted soft and slow outside, muffling the world. Together, they stood at the window, staring into the forest where blue light pulsed and faded like an ancient heart beating in the dark.

For now, the night belonged to them.

***

When the last ember in the false fire dimmed, the night folded around them like a secret, carrying their laughter, their warmth, and the echo of blue light into the waiting dark.

Far beyond the glass, between the trees heavy with snow, something stirred. A lantern swayed once, casting an eerie glow that did not belong to Solstice nor legend. The forest held its breath.

Neither Saree nor Levi spoke of it, but they both felt it—the beginning of something larger than themselves, larger than this night.

Happy Solstice, indeed.

THE END

ACKNOWLEDGEMENTS

To my parents and my brother—thank you for always believing in me, even before I believed in myself. Your support is the quiet magic that carries me through every chapter.

To my friends, who cheer, listen, and talk me off ledges both real and imagined—you are the warmth in my winters.

To my readers—thank you for taking my hand and following me into the snowy forest. For trusting the shadows, embracing the wonder, and letting these stories live beyond my mind. You are the reason this world breathes.

To the incredibly talented team at MiblArt, who once again delivered a breath-taking cover and captured the soul of this tale—thank you for bringing my visions to life with such artistry.

To my wonderful beta readers—your insights, honesty, and enthusiasm strengthened this story in all the right ways. I'm deeply grateful for the care you put into these pages.

And to my amazing street team, ARC team, and every single one of you who shout about these books, share them, recommend them, or simply curl up with them on a quiet night—thank you. Your excitement is the spark that keeps this world alight.

Here's to legends, lantern light, and every brave heart who steps into the dark with me.

www.ingramcontent.com/pod-product-compliance
Lightning Source LLC
Chambersburg PA
CBHW010305100726
47904CB00011B/2760